This book belongs to

....

Written by Hayley Down.
Illustrated by Clare Fennell.

"What's a Christmas?"

Hayley Down · Clare Fennell

make
believe
ideas

As the sun set on Christmas Eve,
a sound BOOMED across the South Pole.

CRASH!

Four little penguins walked along

and tumbled

into a giant

hole!

There, inside that snowy pit, was a funny-shaped snowy mound with two skinny legs sticking out and flippers that made a sound.

"What a weird bird," said Penguin Peg.

"That's no bird!" said Penguin Paul.

"Give it a poke!" said Penguin Pru.

Penguin Pete said nothing at all.

Then something small burst out and cried,
"I'm no bird. I'm Ed the ELF!
I fell out of Santa's Christmas sleigh –
now I've crashed and hurt myself!"

The penguins felt bad for little Ed,
but they were also a bit confused.
They asked:

"What's an elf?"

"What's a sleigh?"

"What's a Santa?"

"What's a Christmas?
And are you
bruised?"

"Oh, bloomin' baubles!" shouted Ed.
"You've never heard of Christmas Day?
I'll teach you how to celebrate
'til Santa returns in his sleigh!"

"First, some sparkle is what we need
to bring some holiday glee."

"Let's try to find some twinkly treats
we can hang on a Christmas tree."

But in the snow, it's hard to find
decorations to gleam and shine,

so what the penguins used instead

were fish

and some boring,

old twine!

Ed said, "Next we'll get **kind gifts** to show our **friends** that we **care**."

"But remember, they should be thoughtful,
not just fancy, sparkly, or rare."

The **gift** they found for their mother
was **cute**, but it wasn't quite **right**;
it was much too **wet**,
much, **MUCH** too **big**,
and it gave her a little
fright!

Next the penguins tried a carol,
and though Ed sang with a smile,

the penguins' horrid, screeching squawks could be heard for miles and miles!

"We've done it **wrong!**" said Penguin Pete.

"We've **ruined** Christmas!" cried out Paul.

Ed said, "I don't know what you **mean**

because I'm having a **ball!**"

"This Christmas may not be fancy,

but the spirit we have is right.

Let's laugh and sing and just be glad

we're together this Christmas night!"

But then Ed's golden pocket watch struck twelve with a jingly chime.

"Oh, no! The sleigh is almost here, and I haven't made a sign!"

His penguin pals knew what to do; they had thought of the perfect gift!

They called all their friends and family to make a sign in the snowdrift . . .

Santa flew over in his sleigh and from way up high, he could see some writing in the snow that said . . .

SANTA, RESCUE.

As Santa landed with a THUD,

he cried out, "Well, what a sight!

I'll spend the rest of Christmas here –

it's the perfect end to my night!"

They celebrated together
and when it was time to say good-bye,
Ed promised that next Christmas . . .

he would be sure to **drop** by!

The end